BABIES, BABIES Everywhere!

Look out for me every time you turn a page!

Words by
Mary Hoffman

Pictures by
Ros Asquith

Otter-Barry BOOKS

We see babies all around us.
In buggies and prams,
in slings and carriers.

For Dylan Wall, with love MH
For Theo, Olympia and Atalanti RA

This book talks about the first year in babies' lives, but not all
babies do the same things at the same age.
Mary (who never did master balancing)
and Ros (who didn't walk till she was eighteen months old)

Text copyright © Mary Hoffman 2021
Illustrations copyright © Ros Asquith 2021
First published in Great Britain in 2021 and in the USA in 2022 by
Otter-Barry Books, Little Orchard, Burley Gate, Herefordshire, HR1 3QS
www.otterbarrybooks.com

A catalogue record for this book is available from the British Library.

ISBN 978-1-91307-470-8

Illustrated with watercolour

Set in Molly Sans Serif

Printed in China

9 8 7 6 5 4 3 2 1

When babies are new,
they can't do much.

They sleep   and they drink milk

and they burp – and of course they pee and poo!

One thing they are VERY good at is crying.

Waaah!

Babies HOWLING everywhere!

They can't talk, so they use crying to mean everything.

After just a few weeks babies can smile.

They giggle when you tickle them.

Tickly wickly Woo!

You mean Tickly wickly WEE!

They wave their arms and legs in the air.

PEEPO

A few weeks later, babies can see faces properly.

They know their mums and dads
and the people they see
every day.

Babies can grasp things with their hands,
like rattles and toys,

and even their own feet!

Baby's better at
toe-touching than
you are.

They coo. . .

coo coo

ba ba ba

and gurgle.

Babies BUBBLING everywhere!

They start to roll over on their playmats.

And soon they can sit up
without help.

After about six months of just milk, babies are ready to try something solid.

Some have a few teeth and can chew on a hard biscuit.

And they can try mushy things.

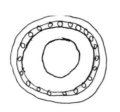

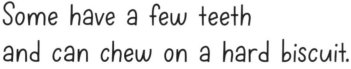

At first they don't know
what to do with their food.

If they have a *go* with a spoon
now, it may be very messy,

but some food
ends up in their
mouths.

Babies'
FOOD
everywhere!

When they start to crawl,
babies can go quite fast.

Some prefer to shuffle along on their bottoms.

Then they start to pull themselves up
to stand, by holding on to chairs.

And soon they are walking
round the room, holding
on to the furniture.

Beware, beware —
there are
babies
everywhere!

By now babies can say a few words. "Mama," "Dada," and "baba" are top favourites.

If they have big brothers and sisters, babies try to say their names too.

Ma ma

Babies BABBLING everywhere!

And they say "more" and "again." Because babies love to do the same things over and over.

One day the baby who holds on to a
chair finds she can stand on her own!
She might be a bit wobbly at first –
it's very different from crawling.

Hooray!

Babies are now on the way to getting around fast.

Off you go, babies!

And now they can walk!

One foot in front of the other,
arms out for balance,
and there's still a lot of falling over.

It's called "toddling".

Get up and try again, babies!

What a lot of things happen
in a baby's first year!
They start as sleepy, cuddly bundles
and soon they are walking,
talking little people.

And now...
they are not babies any more –
they're toddlers.